Red, Yellow, Green...
What Do Signs Mean?

by Joan Holub

For Grace, Sonia, and Edie

D1495949

Copyright © 1998 by Joan Holub.
All rights reserved. Published by Scholastic Inc.
CARTWHEEL BOOKS and the CARTWHEEL BOOKS logo
are trademarks and/or registered trademarks of Scholastic Inc.

ISBN 0-590-13455-8

10 9 8 7 6 5 4 3 2 1

Printed in the U.S.A.   39
First printing, February 1998

Cartwheel
·B·O·O·K·S·®

SCHOLASTIC INC.

New York   Toronto   London   Auckland   Sydney

Red signs, yellow signs,
blue signs, green,
orange, black, brown…
What do they mean?

Signs can help to keep us safe,
or say which way to go.
Signs can tell you where you are,
when to go fast, when to go slow!

There are many sign stickers
in this book. Peel them and
stick them where you find
a match.

Red lights and signs
mean STOP! STOP! STOP!
Don't drive. Don't walk.
Don't run. Don't hop.

This yellow light means CAUTION.
Here comes the red.

Look *all* ways at green lights
before you GO ahead.

A red circle with a line
means NO! NO! NO!
No swimming! No skating!
No dogs in tow!

These yellow signs mean
walkers, bikers, cattle, deer,
or children may be crossing here.

WATCH OUT for moving railroad trains
where this yellow sign is found.

When you see this yellow sign,
there are children playing all around.

These helpful green signs show where you can hike or where you'll find a path for your bike.

Picnic tables and sailboats
are sure to be in sight
near these signs
that are brown and white.

Finding a hospital
should not be hard to do.
Just look for the white "H"
on a background of blue.

Handicapped access
is found anywhere
you see this blue sign
with the white wheelchair.

Orange signs may tell you that workers are nearby fixing streets or bridges or buildings way up high.

elevators

These signs lead to stairs
and to elevators
or to the UP and DOWN escalators.

If you need a little help
when trying to decide
which rest room *you* should enter
let these signs be your guide.

You can make your own signs
and use them anywhere
to say: "MY ROOM!" or "MY TOYS,"
or to tell someone you care.